Big and Little

Jacob Cesaro

Rigby

Contents

Is it big?
Is it little?

3

This cat is big.

This cat is little.

Is it big?
Is it little?

This fish is big.

This fish is little.

Is it big?
Is it little?

This turtle is big.

This turtle is little.

Is it big?
Is it little?

This horse is big.

This horse is little.

Is it big?
Is it little?

11

This lizard is big.

This lizard is little.

Is it big?
Is it little?

13

This bird is big.

This bird is little.

14

Is it big?
Is it little?

This dog is big.

This dog is little.